How To Train Your Ender Dragon - Blind Trust

Funny Comics

Other Books In This Series:

How To Train Your Ender Dragon

Special Bonus

Be sure to read to the back of the book for information on how to get FREE Kindle comics from Funny Comics!

Be sure to “LIKE” our Funny Comics Facebook Page by clicking below

https://www.facebook.com/FunnyComics3000

Subscribe to Funny Comic’s YouTube channel here

Funny Comics YouTube Channel

https://www.youtube.com/channel/UC61rZRtwDl79igc5ltb1Hcg/videos

Be sure to watch our epic Star Wars / Minecraft Mashup “Attack On The Death Square!”

Chapter 1 – *More* Training?!

Apparently, just spending eleven days with your newly hatched dragon is not enough to be able to bond with them fully.

Hey, all. This is Steve again and this time, I'd like to share with you what I'm calling *'training your Ender Dragon adventures'*. Because, like I said... what I went through previously was actually just the initiation phase. Mavrose and I, for all that we are now dragon and rider, are hardly the strongest of pairs.

If you remember, the last time I told you about how I entered the world of Minecraft and ended up choosing Mavrose as my dragon. Now, what you may or may not know is that Ender Dragons are some of the fiercest ones out there – they are powerful, they are strong, and most importantly, they are *opinionated* creatures who will not step down in the face of adversity.

And because of their arrogance and refusal to back off, they are often misunderstood as terrifying creatures of destruction. You saw for yourself the reactions I received when Mavrose hatched for me; they didn't think I would last the first phase of training. Fortunately for me, I did.

CAN I TRUST YOU?

What I didn't know was that there was a secondary aspect to it, which was triggered into action the moment I returned to Minecraft after training ended. Remember how I was told that if I were to stay in Minecraft, my dragon would first have to accept me during training? Well, what Tiamat neglected to tell me was that after my dragon had accepted me, I would have to go through a period of emotional bonding with her to tie us together completely. The first phase of training, if you noticed, was focused entirely on building the physical strengths of dragon and rider. The second would cement the bond between them, allowing them to become partners in full.

Which, as a condition, is all well and good – *unless* you're bonded to an Ender Dragon.

Ender Dragons are not really known for their emotional strengths or their sympathy. They're more likely to eat you than lick your face in happiness.

Fun fact – if I failed phase two of my training... that is, if Mavrose and I ended up not bonding completely, I would be sent back to the real world, memories wiped. I did not want to go back – my brother and his stupid gang were waiting to torment me day and night!

So I set out to do what I had to – emotionally bond to the toughest, meanest, strongest dragon of the lot.

As you can guess, it was either the stupidest or the bravest thing I've ever done. And I've done a *lot* of stupid things.

Chapter 2 – News of the Not Nice Kind

Phase two of Mavrose's training began the very next day after Tiamat decided that I could stay and be part of Minecraft. It was a new beginning for me and I was pumped! That morning, Soaban came to wake us himself. Mavrose was fast asleep on her bed and I was snoring away to glory when he entered our quarters.

He awoke me first by tapping me lightly with his big talon. I jumped up in surprise, but he just rumbled out a small laugh and then wished me good morning before breaking the news to me.

"Morning, Soaban," I mumbled, yawning. Mavrose was still asleep; out of the corner of my eyes, I saw that she was puffing out smoke every time she exhaled out. A small grumbling noise accompanied each breath and if I hadn't gotten used to her by now, I would have certainly been terrified of the fearsome picture she painted even when she was dead to the world.

"Wake your dragon, child," Soaban told me; his eyes were twinkling in a rather disturbing manner and I frowned. "Once the both of you are prepared for the day, come out to the yard. There are other riders eager to meet you, and then you must begin the second half of your training."

I blinked in surprise.

"*Second* half?" I asked, "Didn't I already complete training Mavrose? Training just ended yesterday, didn't it?!"

Soaban shook his long head. "Not quite, child," he said, "Your initial training to ensure that your dragon stayed your own commenced. You completed that quite nicely and you proved to all of us that you have what it takes to be a Minecrafter. But there is more."

I groaned, flopping back on to the bed. "What now?" I muttered and Soaban chuckled.

"You managed to get your dragon trained enough to carry you," he said warmly. "That was an accomplishment of itself. But being partnered with a dragon means more than just having to ride them whenever you feel like it. Mavrose shares your mind, does she not?"

I nodded, squinting up at him. "So?" I knew I sounded petulant, but honestly, who would want *more* training?! Wasn't eleven days being trapped on an island with a grumpy dragon enough?

YOUR FIRST TASK IS TO WAKE YOUR DRAGON CHILD ...

THAT DOESN'T SOUND EASY ...

ZZZZZZ...ooo

"There is an emotional aspect to every bond, especially when it comes to that of a dragon and its rider," Soaban told me seriously. "Mavrose has accepted you as a trainer and rider, but that does not mean that things are perfect. You must connect with each other and become partners in full or you will not be able to succeed here in Minecraft."

"So what, I have to like become all *emo* around her now?" I moaned. Soaban laughed – it sounded like thunder rumbling in the distance, but I guess that's what being a dragon is like.

"You can start by waking her up," he responded. "That will be your first test. You will need to understand her and learn to anticipate her. And with an Ender Dragon... that is... well, it's not exactly *easy*."

He cast a meaningful look at my dragon. On cue, Mavrose growled a little in her sleep, a puff of smoke escaping her large nostrils, and I narrowed my eyes at her. Anticipate her? Great. I could anticipate her wanting to eat me, certainly, but not letting me into her mind or sharing her '*emotions*' with me.

We were *so* doomed.

"I must warn you child," Soaban's voice turned low and serious, "If you do not manage to bond fully with your dragon, we will send you back home with your memories wiped. Minecraft has little place for a dragon and rider not properly paired."

"And how will we know that we *have* been trained fully?" I snarked back at him. He didn't answer, turning around, and walked out, his tail swishing back and forth behind him. I just stared after him for a long moment, contemplating my life.

Seriously?

What did I even do to deserve this?! More training?

Or else go back home to where those monkeys were, just ready to torment me day in and day out.

Like I *really* had a choice.

With a sigh, I jumped off my bed and then went to do as Soaban had instructed.

I just had to wake a grumpy but powerful Ender Dragon who liked to roast things more than she liked to make friends. What could *possibly* go wrong?

Chapter 3 – My Dragon Roasts, Mistakes Me for Bacon

Apparently a *lot* of things could go wrong.

Let's start with the fact that Mavrose thought I was her breakfast and nearly fried me to death.

I walked over to where she was fast asleep and stood there, breathing in deeply. Mavrose didn't frighten me exactly, but she *was* intimidating. Big and black, she was one of the strongest dragons out there and as her trainer, I was intimately aware of just *how* strong she really was.

So being the clever guy that I am, I stepped back a few inches and then called for her to wake up instead of touching her.

Which turned out to be a pretty good idea, since the stupid dragon sneezed and nearly killed me.

It happened like this.

"Mavrose?" I called softly, "Mavrose, wake up. Soaban has work for us to do. Wake up, dude, c'mon."

I DIDN'T THINK THIS WOULD BE EASY, YOUCH!

(Okay, not my best moment, calling my grumpy female dragon *dude*, but some instincts don't go away, alright?!)

"Mavrose, c'mon, wake up," I pleaded and in response, my dragon just snorted. Flames shot out of her snout – big, scary flames that were tinged black and that were *super* hot.

I jumped out of the way, yelping in shock, as the jet of fire just raced past the spot that I was standing at. A moment later and I would have been incinerated.

Oh and the stupid dragon was *still* sleeping.

Growling, I stomped back to her and started yelling.

"Mavrose, you *idiot*!" I screamed, "You nearly killed me. Would just wake up already?!"

Another snort and another jet of flame.

"Hmmmm..." the rumble was in my head and I shrieked a little, startled, before I realized that she was speaking to me. Only, she was still asleep, so she was probably murmuring in her sleep.

(Yes, dragons can reach into their riders' minds when they're sleeping. Yes, we have access to their dreams. No it is most certainly *not* a fun experience. Why? See for yourself.)

"Baaaacccooon..."

Her long, pink tongue fell out and slowly made a circuit around huge, ivory teeth that were sharp and pointed. They were like mini-swords, ready to rip into anything and I felt myself shivering before I realized what she just said.

The dumb dragon was dreaming about food.

She had nearly *fried* me to death because she was dreaming about *bacon.*

That was it.

I stomped over to her and jumped on her, yelling into her ear.

"Wake up, you silly girl!" I cried.

Which, in hindsight, truly was one of the stupidest things I've ever done.

Mavrose startled awake, growling and letting loose a third jet of flame. This one was more a stream than a puff and it blasted right through the roof, even as my blasted dragon growled and twisted to get me off her long, scaly back.

"Mavrose, it's *me*!" I exclaimed into her mind as she roared in anger, shaking every which way and that.

“Stop, Mavrose, it’s Steve!” I cried out loud this time, and she puffed out a jet of smoke before peering up at me on her back suspiciously.

“Steve?” she asked, huge, oval eyes narrowing to small slits.

“Yeah, Mavrose, it’s me!” I yelled. “Now stop acting so irritating and let me get *off*!”

“What in the world are you doing up there in the first place, you puny human?” she grumbled into my mind, before huffing and bending down so I could get off. I clambered down easily, used to her big form after so many days of doing nothing but playing around with her.

“I was trying to wake you up,” I muttered, rocking back and forth on my ankles, suddenly embarrassed. I was beginning to realize that that may *not* have been the best way to do so.

“And you thought jumping on top of me was how to do it?” she asked incredulously. “Are you out of your mind?!”

“No,” I answered sulkily, “*You* would know. You’re *in* my mind.”

She growled, snapping at me with her snout and I dodged it, smirking at her. She just huffed and laid back down, closing her eyes.

"Oh no, you don't," I said, reaching out to rub her hide and slowly dragging my hand down her side. Mavrose was ticklish and that was something I'd discovered during our training. I was not above using it to my advantage at this moment.

(You're probably wondering why I had such difficulty waking her up now when we spent eleven whole days together, training. Thing is, since those days were devoted entirely to physical training, we slept very little. I can honestly remember conking off only a few times and those hours were generally spent apart. Mavrose preferred to sleep close to the waterfalls and for obvious, reasons, I did *not*. This was the first chance I had to actually wake her up.)

"C'mon, you," I bumped her snout and she growled in a low tone, finally giving in and moving her big butt.

"Alright, alright," she grumbled, "I'm awake, human. You don't need to be such an annoying gnat."

I glared at her. She nearly *roasted* me to death on our first day in Minecraft and *I* was the annoying gnat?

Just then, a few pieces of drywall and hay fell on my head and I looked up. Right above where Mavrose was, there was a humungous hole, right through the roof, about a foot in diameter.

I stared at it incredulously before I groaned loudly.

My dragon mistook me for bacon and tried to roast me and in the process, ended up putting a gorgeous skylight in the roof that was my quarters, gifted to us by none other than the Shahleigh.

Oh yeah, my training was off to an *amazing* start.

Chapter 4 – New Friends Come Along with New Challenges

Once Mavrose was awake, we went over to the arena that Soaban had asked me to come to. I was getting quite hungry by this time and I was looking forward to breakfast.

All three of the Shahleigh were waiting for us just outside the dining hall. Soaban greeted us with a friendly growl and then Tiamat ruffled my hair with her talons (which, if you're not used to dragons, can be quite scary). My mind, though, was busy worrying about the implications of the hole we'd burnt right through the roof. As we walked inside, Tiamat noticed my distraction and came closer to me.

"Are you alright, child?" she murmured softly. "You look worried."

I shook my head awkwardly, wondering how I should tell her. I shuffled my weight from foot to foot, shooting her sheepish smiles.

"Um... Mavrose burnt a hole through the ceiling of our quarters when I was trying to wake her up!" I blurted out. "It-it wasn't *my* fault, *she* was dreaming about bacon and nearly *killed* me-"

"Thank you, human," Mavrose hissed into my mind and her big eyes narrowed into displeased slits as she glared at me, growling and puffing out warning smoke. I winced, sighing... I was *so* doomed.

Bazr blinked. For a moment, there was utter silence and I braced myself, getting ready for punishment, when all of a sudden, Tiamat started laughing, a low rumbling sound in her belly. A second later, Soaban joined her and before I knew it, all three of the Shahleigh were laughing and I was just standing there, an incredulous look on my face.

They were not angry!

But Mavrose was annoyed with me and I was definitely going to pay for selling her out later. The knowledge had me gulping even as Tiamat moved forward and breathed a warm puff of smoke on my hair.

"These things happen, child," she chuckled, "We shall send one of the Minecrafters to fix your roof."

"Do be careful the next time, though," Bazr added. "We cannot keep breaking and fixing things constantly."

I nodded, sighing in relief. "Of course," I bowed my head and then followed them inside the dining hall.

Before I could step in, however, Mavrose caught me by placing a single talon inside my shirt and yanking me back. I yelped in surprise, the sharp edge of her claw scraping my skin lightly and turned around to glare at her.

"What?" I snapped. She puffed out more warning smoke.

"I will not let this go, human," she growled into my mind. I knew she could see how intimidated by her I was, but I still put on a brave face anyway, shrugging as nonchalantly as I could.

"They needed to know," I insisted. "And *you* were the one who broke the roof, not me."

With that, I marched inside, leaving behind an irritated, grumpy Ender Dragon to glare after me.

The dining hall was kind of a buffet, really. There were a few tables set to the side for the riders to sit and eat, but from what I could see, there were very few of them present. Only one or two people were eating at the tables; the rest of them seemed to just get the food and walk through a stone archway to somewhere else.

Mavrose, huffing, decided not to stick with me and instead just stalked down the hall to the archway and went straight through it. She seemed to know where it led to, but I ignored her, walking up to where the food was and pulling out a square-shaped plate.

As I collected my food and pulled out some forks and knives, a young girl saddled up to me, offering me a bright grin. She was really pretty, with long red hair that flipped over her shoulders as she smiled at me.

“Hello, you must be Steve!” she chirped and I blinked in surprise.

“Uh, hi?” I responded, confused. How did she know who I was?

“I’m Robyn,” she introduced herself. “We’re so excited to finally meet the guy who trained an Ender Dragon, that too all by himself!”

I stared at her with a puzzled look on my face and she laughed, grabbing my elbow and leading me down the archway that Mavrose had gone through. I followed her, only to find myself in a large clearing where the other riders were sitting, propped up against their dragons, eating their breakfast. It struck me then that they preferred to hang out with their dragons.

Oh *yay*.

Meanwhile, *my* dragon was busy being a whiny, grumpy baby. I sighed, following Robyn to where her dragon was.

“This is Baya,” she introduced us and I stared at her in awe. Baya wasn’t as impressive as Mavrose was the first time I saw her (Mavrose *is* an Ender Dragon, after all), but she was still quite intimidating. Her emerald scales shone bright in the sunlight and she puffed out long breaths of smoke as she bent down to touch her snout to my forehead in a friendly greeting.

"Hello there, Steve," her voice was soft and melodious and her big eyes twinkled merrily as she leaned over to give her rider a friendly lick.

"H-hi," I stuttered. From the distance, I could hear a low, angry growl and I turned to see that Mavrose was just a few feet away, snarling and glaring at me. Robyn jumped at the sound, hazel eyes going wide at the sight of my dragon.

"Th-that's... oh *my*!" she breathed and I was startled to realize that she was shaking from fright.

"That's my dragon," I told her, trying to make my voice as reassuring as possible. "Her name is Mavrose."

"She's an Ender Dragon," Robyn whispered. I frowned.

"I thought you knew that...?" I pointed and she nodded timidly.

WOW, AN ENDER DRAGON!
THIS IS MAVROSE

"Yes but..." she continued to stare at Mavrose, who stalked closer, tail swishing predatorily. I rolled my eyes; since when did my dragon become such an attention seeker?

"Don't worry," I muttered. "She won't hurt you."

I paused, considering it. "Much," I added as an afterthought. Robyn yelped and I chuckled, shaking my head.

"Kidding," I whispered and she offered me a brief glare. Mavrose came to stand close to me, still growling and I sighed, plopping down on the ground next to Baya, who was watching my dragon warily.

"Mavrose, this is Baya and her rider, Robyn," I introduced them, leaning against Baya, who dropped an emerald-scaled wing over me. Mavrose's eyes narrowed.

"It is nice to meet you," she said stiffly. Robyn just stared at her with eyes spread wide in awe and then jumped up, nodding furiously.

"Y-yes," she squealed breathlessly. "It's *so* great to meet you, oh my *god*!"

"Finish your breakfast quickly, Steve," Mavrose muttered stiffly. "We must begin training as soon as we can."

Before I could reply though, she turned around and stomped off, puffing smoke irritably. I glared after, throwing my food into my mouth and chewing harshly. I felt Baya's skin vibrate beneath me and I shot her a questioning look. Robyn sighed, sitting down next to me and Baya just snorted an amused puff of smoke.

"Your dragon is certainly interesting," she murmured. I exhaled in a rush, wondering what was so funny about a grumpy dragon. Shrugging, I quickly finished my breakfast as Mavrose had ordered and then bid them both farewell.

"I'll see you guys later," I told them, shaking hands with Robyn and offering Baya a quick rub of her snout. Robyn nodded and Baya licked my hand.

"Have a good day," she chirped and I waved goodbye as I got up. I disposed of the plate in the bin where the dishes were left to be washed later and then went out to the middle of the clearing, where Mavrose was lying curled up in the sun.

"I see you *finally* decided to join me," she snapped and I glared at her.

"It's not like I was dancing around and having fun," I retorted. "I *do* need to eat."

She huffed and then slowly got up, stretching her long neck and letting loose a small jet of flame into the sky.

All around us, the noise suddenly vanished and I was embarrassed to realize that the other riders had stopped whatever they were doing to stare at us. An Ender Dragon can be a thing of absolute beauty, even when she's being a grumpy baby and a part of me was extremely proud to call her my dragon.

(Of course, I wasn't going to let *her* know that, though she may have already read it in my mind. Still, I was keeping my mouth tightly shut. I don't need her getting any more vain. Or whiny. Or grumpy. See the pattern here?)

Mavrose looked down at me smugly. I sighed, ignoring her, just as the Shahleigh approached us.

"Are you ready, Minecrafter Steve?" Tiamat asked formally and I took a deep breath, nodding.

"Tell me what we must do," I answered determinedly and Bazr nodded approvingly.

"Trust between dragon and rider is important," Soaban repeated what he'd told me earlier. "In fact, it is the most essential thing of all. You need to be able to trust that your dragon will always come when you call and she needs to know that you will not abandon her when she requires your aid."

"So, for today," Tiamat took over, "We shall perform a simple exercise. You will be blindfolded and your dragon bound. Reaching out with your mind, you must find her and follow your link to her."

"You must trust that *she* will direct you to where she is without letting you get hurt," Bazr added. "And Mavrose must not try to get herself unbound before you reach her. She must trust that *you* will find her and let her loose."

Blindfolded? Following *directions*?

Fear prickled my spine and I could tell that my dragon was also uneasy. It wasn't that we didn't trust each other – we had spent eleven whole days together, getting ourselves physically fit enough to be dragon and rider. However, losing our senses and relying on each other for the sensations... that was a new one, and it wasn't one I was comfortable with in the least.

"Blindfolded?" I sputtered. "Bu-but... that's..."

"Are you not willing to trust your dragon, child?" there was an uneasy tinge to Tiamat's voice and it straightened my resolve.

"If you do not wish to do this, you need only say so and we will return you to your realm." Soaban's voice held a note of finality.

Honestly? I really, *really* didn't want to do this. I did care for my dragon, and on good days, I even liked her. But to let myself be so vulnerable and trust that she would guide me to safety...? It was a daunting prospect. Mavrose felt the same, I could tell.

But the alternative was to return to the real world, where my tormentors were waiting... where I was not Minecrafter Steve who rode the might Ender Dragon, but just an average school kid who had absolutely nothing special about him.

I took a deep breath.

"Mavrose?" I murmured into her mind. She puffed out an irritated breath before nodding.

"We're ready," I looked straight at the Shahleigh, stiffening my back and looking determined.

"Then go forth, child," Tiamat smiled.

And it was on.

Chapter 5 – I Learn to Swim Blindfolded

The training session was an *utter* disaster.

And I am not even exaggerating.

Here's what happened.

Tiamat sent me back to the arena with Bazr, who handed me a golden ring. When I asked him what it was for, he told me that it would block my connection to Mavrose for the whole day so that I wouldn't instinctively know where she was being taken. It was only then that I realized – ever since I'd come to Minecraft, I knew *exactly* where my dragon was every second of every day. Her presence in my mind was constant – a sort of a low buzz that was as comforting as it could be irritating.

The moment I put on the ring, though, she vanished from my mind. I was pretty shaken up at the sensation; even though she was right there and I could see her with my own eyes, I couldn't feel her mind.

I didn't realize how dependent I'd become on the feel of her mind until it was taken away from me.

Robyn, who was still eating with Baya, noticed the stricken look on my face. The emerald dragon slowly got up and came over to me, offering me a comforting lick with a long, barbed tongue. From the corner of my eye, I saw Mavrose huff out a puff of irritated smoke before Soaban led her away and suddenly, my dragon and I were *too* far apart.

Bazr patted my shoulder comfortingly with his own wing.

“Have faith, child,” he told me kindly. “Trust that you and your dragon will find one another.”

I breathed in deeply and then nodded, rolling the ring between my fingers. Twenty minutes later, Robyn hugged me, wished me good luck and then I was following Bazr into a small room to the side of the arena, where I was to get ready.

(Which is basically a euphemistic way of saying that they were going to make me blind, but who’s complaining?)

Ten minutes after that, I was dressed in these strange breeches and tunic that Bazr said would provide me with some basic protection against the elements. I was about to ask him what in the world he meant when the blindfold was tied tightly around my eyes and I was lumped on to Bazr’s back.

I shrieked as the dragon took off – while it’s now instinctive for me to ride a dragon after eleven days of training to do just that, *that* instinct works only when

I'm with Mavrose. Bazr was smaller, his shape slightly different from my own dragon, and I was startled to realize how much I relied on not just my sight, but also my own body to be able to ride Mavrose so flawlessly.

Bazr dropped me off at the edge of the woods.

"Good luck, child," he intoned in a deep voice, breathing a puff of hot air over my hair. "I hope you succeed."

With that, I felt the whoosh of his wings as he took off.

Fear clogged my throat as I suddenly became *terrified.* I couldn't see a single thing and I was standing in a place that was utterly alien to me! I doubted that I could even find my way in my own room back home – I knew that inside out and I was sure I couldn't do it blindfolded like this! How in the *world* was I supposed to make my way through a whole forest that I'd *never* stepped into before?!

Gulping and shaking, I remembered that Bazr asked me to remove the ring once I was ready to start my challenge. I scrambled to do, yanking the thing off my hands like it was burning and with frightened tears in my eyes, I reached out with my mind instinctively, looking for my dragon.

“Mavrose?” I called out, both in my mind and out loud. My voice echoed within the forest, bouncing back to me in a strange, loud imitation of my fear and I swallowed hard.

“*MAVROSE*!” I begged, tugging at the blindfold. The stupid thing wouldn’t give; apparently, the Shahleigh had magicked it on to me. “Mavrose, I need you!”

I could feel a distant buzz at the back of my mind that was the presence of my dragon. I almost sobbed out in relief, latching on to our connection and opening my mind to her fully –

Only to hit a big, blank wall as she refused to respond to me.

“Mavrose?!” I called again. “Please, dude, c’mon. *We* need to do this. I can't see, I need you to direct me!”

She still didn’t reply.

“*Mavrose*, I know you’re bound too,” I tried again, “Let me help! Direct me so that I can find you and unbind you. *Please*, Mavrose...”

My Ender Dragon refused to answer.

It wasn’t that she couldn’t feel me – I *knew* she could, given that the annoying buzz at the back of my mind was becoming stronger and stronger by the minute. For some reason, Mavrose just would not talk to me.

"*MAVROSE*!" I yelled, "Will just speak to me already?! We don't have all day! You're *bound* and I'm *blind*, we have to help each other!"

"I don't need a puny human's help!" she shrieked at me and I stumbled back, heart racing as her voice filled my head. Before I could respond to her, she retreated again.

"Have you lost it?" I asked finally. She didn't reply.

After that, no matter how many times I tried to speak to her, she would say a single thing. The buzz in my mind let me know that we were definitely connected, that she could hear me, but she ignored me harder than ever. No matter how much I begged and pleaded, she would not answer.

Now I was just getting plain angry.

Without another word, I closed my eyes (not that it made any difference, since I couldn't see), and focused on the buzz. For as long as I'd been with Mavrose, I'd known where she was without having to see her, so I was hoping that this connection would quietly lead me to her.

Even if said dragon was being an annoying, irritating... in her own words, '*gnat*'. I was going to flay her alive when I found her, but find her I would.

I concentrated as hard as I could, trying to pinpoint her location. The buzz grew louder and louder, till it blocked out everything else, till it was all I could hear and feel.

There!

Shouting in triumph, I jumped up and took off in the direction that I knew Mavrose was in. The connection was leading me straight to her – I could almost see the silver line that I was following, that I knew would bring me to my dragon.

The thing is, I was seeing it with my mind's eye. I'd forgotten in my excitement that my *actual* eyes were darkened, that I couldn't see anything. And I was concentrating so much on the buzz inside my head that I ignored all the other sensations I felt, from the rough terrain to the gurgling sound of water next to me.

Too late, I heard it – Mavrose shrieking in my head.

"STEVE, NO!"

IS THAT WATER I HEAR? I CAN'T SEE A THING!

I fell straight into the river, flailing about like a madman, water gushing into my open mouth and nose as I sputtered and coughed. Tears burned my eyes, but I couldn't breathe or see – swimming is a hundred times harder when you've lost your vision.

"STEVE!"

Mavrose was yelling in my head, and distantly, I could feel her trying to get to me. But it was of no use – she was bound and could not move.

"NO, NO, NO! STEVE!"

I coughed, thrashing my skinny arms and legs as I tried to keep afloat. The current was too strong for me, however and I was drowning. Breathing became difficult and I coughed hard, before I gave in to the inevitable and closed my eyes –

Just to be yanked out by a powerful talon and pulled out into dry land. I sucked in huge gulps of air, grateful to be alive, as I threw up the water I'd swallowed. My stomach and chest hurt as I heaved again and again.

I looked up blearily to see Tiamat watching me worriedly – *wait, I could see again!*

I realized that the blindfold had been taken off.

"Steve!" Mavrose still sounded panicked, but the next thing I knew, she was in front of me, licking me worriedly, even as huge, fat tears gathered in her big eyes.

It took me a long moment to understand just what was going on.

Mavrose hadn't answered my calls and she hadn't directed me to her. So, I being the genius I am, tried to follow my connection straight to her, only to fall face first into the river because I couldn't see.

Tiamat, who had probably judging our training from the outside with the rest of the Shahleigh, had to come save me, because my dragon did not answer.

My dragon did not answer.

And I almost died.

"YOU!" I roared at Mavrose, who shrunk back. (It was a funny sight in retrospect, seeing such a big, scary Ender Dragon look so small.)

"You didn't *answer*!" I yelled and Mavrose hung her head in shame. "You didn't respond to me even after I called for you so many times!"

"Steve, I-" she was perilously close to tears, I could see. "I'm sorry, I just-"

“Save it,” I snapped. “I don’t wanna hear it.”

Without another word, I turned around and stalked off. I wanted to tell her that it was ok, that we could try again, when I saw her tears, but I was too angry.

So I just ignored her and returned to our quarters, where the workmen were fixing the inadvertent skylight Mavrose had made in the morning. I flopped on to the bed and closed my eyes, falling asleep before I knew what was happening.

I was going to give my sulky little Ender Dragon a taste of her own stupid medicine.

Chapter 6 – Dragons have Feelings Too, Apparently

Something strange happened that night.

Mavrose *apologized.*

I know, I am not exaggerating – my Ender Dragon, who is almost *always* sulky and grumpy and whiny, came up to me and *apologized.*

I awoke somewhere around the time that the sun was setting; it cast a bright, pink glow around my quarters and I was surprised to see that Mavrose was curled up in her bed, snorting lowly. She was also asleep, but unlike this morning, she wasn't dreaming happily of breakfast. I sensed unease drifting off her mind, but I slammed my mental walls up – I had no wish to speak to her or soothe her in any way.

Stupid dragon almost got me killed with her stubbornness. I felt fully justified in ignoring her as I got up, yawned and went to find some food.

I winced as my muscles pulled – swimming against the current had really taken a lot out of me, especially since I wasn't all that athletic to begin with! I groaned in a small voice as my legs protested my every step; it seemed like an eternity passed before I was stepping into the dining hall again, eager to get something to eat.

I grabbed a plate and quickly filled it, heading out through the archway, hoping Baya or Robyn would be there. They were.

Baya was flying around the clearing while Robyn sat on a log of wood, dinner in hand. She was watching her dragon with an affectionate expression on her face and suddenly, I was absolutely jealous of her.

She clearly loved her dragon very much.

Baya growled back at her, flapping her wings harder and Robyn laughed out loud, waving to her excitedly.

The green dragon also clearly cared for her a great deal.

I forced a smile on to my face and went over to where the redhead was, sitting down next to her. She greeted me with a soft smile and a friendly punch.

"You alright there, Steve?" she asked quietly. "We heard what happened."

I wanted to die right then and there. Great. *Everyone* knew that my dragon hated me. Could this day get any worse?

Add that to the list of things one never says unless one is not jinxed, because apparently it *could.*

Mavrose suddenly showed up.

I was just recounting the whole story to Robyn in a low tone when my dragon stumbled into the clearing. Given that I had shut off our connection, I hadn't felt her awaken or come in search of me. By this time, Baya had finished her flying session and joined us. I was leaning against her, as was Robyn, and she had one wing spread over us, wrapping us in a warm, cozy, tent-like feeling.

Of course, my crazy dragon just stepped straight up and glared at us.

"Steve," she growled. "Get up."

I glared right back at her.

"Go away, Mavrose," I snapped. "I don't want to speak to you right now."

"Steve, get *up*, or you will regret it," she reached out to snap at Baya, who growled back but pulled her wing away from me nonetheless. The sudden loss of her warmth left me feeling bereft and I jumped up, my eyes shooting daggers at my dragon.

"What do you want, Mavrose?!" I yelled, "Can't you just leave me alone?!"

She stiffened. For a moment, there was nothing but silence.

The next thing I knew, she'd caught me within her massive talons and we were flying over the clearing, heading straight back to our quarters.

"What *the*-?" I shrieked in surprise, hanging on to her for dear life as she weaved her way through the streets.

"*MAVROSE, PUT ME DOWN, YOU INSANE DRAGON!*" I beat my hands against her scales, but it was in vain – she was, literally, too thick skinned for it to make a difference.

"Mavrose, *what* are you doing?" I cried into her mind. She, obviously, ignored me, wings flapping up and down powerfully. "Mavrose, let me *go*!"

For long, shaky minutes, I was carried by my dragon and I was shaking, terrified. I hated heights, as you probably remember, and though I'd gotten better at it since I became a rider, it didn't mean that I enjoyed being carried around like in her talons like eagle-food!

MAVROSE, PUT ME DOWN!

When she finally put me down – gently too – I looked around and realized that she'd brought me to our quarters. The hole in the roof had been enlarged, I saw, into an entry and an exit for when Mavrose could fly to our home.

"Are you *mad*?!" I yelled at her, stomping my foot on the ground. "What in the world is *wrong* with you?!"

"Shut up!" she roared back at me. "If you didn't insist on being so *stupid*, I wouldn't have to behave in such a-"

"Stupid?" I yelped, "STUPID?! *You* were the one who just carried me out of the clearing without warning! *You* were the one who almost let me drown today! *You've* been acting like a grumpy little baby since we first met and-"

"Watch your language, human," she snarled, a warning puff of smoke escaping her nostrils. I ignored her threat, instead yelling straight on – I was too mad to care.

"-I was just hanging out with Robyn and Baya, who seem to appreciate me far more than you and you just barge in-"

"Then maybe next time, you can have *Baya* connect to your mind and hatch for you instead," she cut in cruelly and I stopped yelling, blinking in surprise.

"Baya is- wait, *what*?"

Mavrose turned her back to me and padded over to her bed, where she just curled up and refused to say anything. I walked over to her cautiously, reaching out with my mind to try to understand what she meant.

I froze at the sensations running through her head.

My stupid, silly Ender Dragon was *jealous.*

She was jealous that I connected so easily with Baya and I'd had to struggle to even speak to her properly when we first met.

Affection rushed through me suddenly – I reached out and rubbed her snout comfortingly, pressing a small kiss to the tip.

"*You're* the idiot, Mavrose," I murmured, opening my mind up to her fully. She closed her eyes, nuzzling into my touch as I rested my head against her huge face.

"Don't call me names, human," she purred and I chuckled, the fight draining out of me easily.

One large gemstone eye opened and stared at me in trepidation.

"I'm sorry, Steve," she whispered, her voice broken and sad, "I didn't answer you because I was envious of the way you were curled up with that green dragon. And I was too proud to think that an Ender Dragon like me would need help from a small little creature like you."

I snorted, moving back a little to sit next to her.

"That's the *point*, isn't it, dummy?" I asked softly. "This phase of our training means letting go of our inhibitions and actually trusting each other, no matter how much we don't like it."

Hesitantly, I leaned against her, wondering if she would push me away or turned me into bacon a second time. She responded instantly, dropping a wing over me just like Baya had done earlier.

With Baya, it felt like a privilege, like I was a special guest being given a token of appreciation.

With Mavrose, it felt like coming home.

I sighed quietly, reaching out to rub her wing, and she squirmed, puffing out smoke. I did it again and she swatted at me.

I laughed as I realized – she was extra ticklish there. So I just reached out and poked at her wing a third time and she growled in warning before she puffed a breath of smoke into my face.

I sputtered, coughing and glared at her through watery eyes. She crossed her wings smugly, a red tongue coming out to lick my face in silent apology. I sighed and leaned back against her, looking up through our new skylight at the night sky. The stars were clearly visible and I smiled, at peace with my dragon.

"Think we can try again tomorrow?" I asked her finally.

In response, she breathed out slowly, ruffling my hair with her exhales, and then licked my elbow.

"I know we can," she murmured softly into my mind, before falling asleep like that, with me cuddled into her side.

Maybe the training won't be *so* bad after all.

Chapter 7 – Second Chances Make All the Difference

The next morning went a bit better.

It was Bazr's turn to wake us up today and he seemed quite pleased to see the both of us cuddled up together on Mavrose's bed. There was a hint of unease about him though and I yawned as I got up, wondering what he needed.

"If you don't complete the task today, Steve," he told me mournfully when I asked him, "Then I'm afraid we will have to wipe your memories and send you back. Mavrose will remain an unattached dragon again."

The dragon in question snorted and purred, waking up slowly. She puffed out a small stream of smoke, but fortunately didn't try to turn me into bacon. One large eye pooped open as she offered Bazr a friendly yowl.

"I'm no longer unattached, Bazr," she said firmly. "I made a mistake yesterday. It will not happen a second time."

Bazr blinked, long and slow, before his lips parted in a wide smile.

(A dragon's smile can be both scary and intimidating, believe me. Those big teeth, those large lips and those huge canines...? Yikes!)

"I am happy to hear that," he said, turning around and padding out, pausing just at the door to turn back.

"Please get ready and make your way to the arena as soon as you can," he told us and then disappeared outside, leaving me alone with my Ender Dragon.

I looked up at Mavrose, a warm gush of affection lighting my chest. She blinked back grumpily, though I knew she could feel it in my mind.

"You won't leave me hanging this time...?" I teased her, but I was also well aware that she could sense the quiet trepidation in the back of my mind.

She growled softly, breathing out a hot puff of air over my face.

"Let us go," she answered and I sighed, clambering on to her back as she bunched up her hind muscles, taking off with a powerful jump. Just like that, we are high in the air, the wind rushing past my face as Mavrose's wings flapped on either side of me. It made me feel on top of the world – how many school kids got to experience something as wondrous as this?!

The good feeling lasted all the way through breakfast. Robyn was there again and waved to me as I dismounted from Mavrose in the arena. This time, though, she didn't take off on her own, instead hanging around with me as I grabbed my plate and stalked through the archway into the clearing.

Baya's smile turned stiff at the sight of my dragon following me. Robyn rushed over and hugged me, blabbing worriedly.

"Are you alright? Mavrose just took off with you yesterday and we were *so* worried and I just-"

"Robyn," I laughed, pushing her off, "Relax. It's alright. We just needed to sort things out, we're fine now."

Baya peered down at me with one, large, knowing eye. I met her gaze and offered her a small nod, letting her know that it truly was alright and the tension drained away from her. She bumped her snout against my elbow and then looked up at Mavrose who was watching her guardedly.

Without another word, I pulled my dragon on to the ground with me, curling up against her like I'd done just last night. Silly, possessive dragon... I liked Baya, I *did*, but Mavrose was...*Mavrose*. She was *mine*, she'd hatched for *me* and I'd trained with *her*, not the emerald dragon.

I let her feel all those things in my mind and she sighed softly, dropping a wing against me and tilting her head at Robyn and Baya, who smiled.

ARE YOU READY FOR YOUR FINAL ATTEMPT STEVE?

An hour later, we were chatting away and laughing like old friends. Mavrose finally loosened up, letting go of that stiffness and ego that I think all Ender Dragons possess.

Just then, the Shahleigh approached us. I stood up, wiping my hands on my pants and dusting away the crumbs.

"Are you ready for your second and final try, Minecraft Steve?" Tiamat asked me formally. I looked up to meet Mavrose's knowing gaze, before I turned back to her and nodded determinedly.

"We are," I answered confidently, pushing down the nervous feeling that spurting up at the back of my throat. The tip of Mavrose's wing dragged itself down my elbow and I straightened up – *we were going to get it this time*, I promised myself.

"Then let us begin," Soaban muttered and handed me the golden ring again. Robyn hugged me, wishing me good luck and Baya offered me a farewell lick on my elbow. I turned to Mavrose, who bent her long snout over me and let me hug her face.

"I trust you," I murmured into her ear. A single film of liquid shone on her eyelid and I was startled to realize that she had tears in her eyes as she growled her confirmation.

"And I you," she whispered in my mind before she took off after Tiamat and Bazr. Soaban led me to the small room again and let me get ready. I put on the ring and breathed in sharply as the buzz in my head ceased to exist.

It was on.

Chapter 8 – My 'Blind' Trust in my Dragon Pays Off

This time, we did *spectacularly*.

Mavrose and I were perfectly in sync. Soaban dropped me off at the edge of the woods again, wishing me luck before he took off. I couldn't see anything as I removed the ring from my finger.

And there she was.

The buzz at the back of my mind returned, but with it, I could hear Mavrose's voice, whispering my name quietly.

"Steve?"

"I'm here," I answered and I smiled as I felt the returning rush of relief from her. Quickly, I opened my mind to her fully and stumbled back in giddy joy as I felt her do the same. This time, we were *not* going to fail.

Because this time, we were in *full* harmony with one another the way a dragon and her trainer ought to be.

"How do I get to you?" I asked, putting one step in front of the other, hands out cautiously searching for anything that might harm me. Distantly, I could feel it as Mavrose closed her own eyes and opened her senses to mine. As an Ender Dragon, she was in sync with the forest and the elements, so she'd be able to tell me if I was in any kind of danger.

"Keep walking as you are right now," she instructed me, "Go for ten paces before turning to your left."

I followed her instructions carefully. Each step I took brought me closer to her, but more importantly, the stiffness in my gait and the overly cautious and careful manner with which I began slowly vanished. I could trust Mavrose; she would not lead me wrong. She would make sure I made it to her safe and sound – the knowledge sank into my chest and before I knew it, I was utterly relaxed and happy, as though I was simply taking a stroll through the woods on a sunny day.

Suddenly though, Mavrose yelled sharply in my head.

"Steve, stop!"

I froze, throwing my hands up in defense. Mavrose sighed in my head.

"In front of you is a huge tree," she said softly, "Reach out with your hands, you should be able to feel it."

THERE IS A TREE IN FRONT OF YOU STEVE!

Very, very carefully, I put out my hand, reaching out to see if she was being honest. Suddenly, I jerked back – my fingers came into contact with something hard and tawny and slightly damp. I knew it was wood, probably the bark of a tree.

I exhaled lightly, the blood pounding through my veins and my head spinning slightly. I breathed out in relief – Mavrose did care, after all. It made me smile wider than ever. Nearby I could hear the gurgle of the river I'd fallen into the last time and I chuckled as I reached out with my mind to my dragon.

"Now?" I asked, waiting for her direction. It didn't take long.

"Take two steps to your left," she answered immediately, "You'll be able pass through without trouble."

I did as she told me to, and true to her words, I walked past unscathed, pushing on towards where she was waiting for me.

This pattern continued for over two-three hours; I walked down what felt like the entire forest, with Mavrose directing me in my mind. I trusted her completely and utterly.

But I was also worried for her. I could feel that the bonds were chaffing away at her scales, even as she tried to ignore the pain to help me. It wasn't until then that I realized what being bound meant; she wasn't just tied up, she was also hurting.

It made me walk faster so that I could release her.

Ender Dragons are proud creatures, even arrogant at times. So it didn't come as a surprise when Mavrose didn't even mention how much she was hurting. Fortunately, given that the connection was wide open, I could feel her pain, just as she could feel me.

Soon enough, I was right in front of where she was tied up. The blindfold fell away on its own and I slowly opened my eyes, squinting against the sudden, harsh light to see my dragon lying down on the floor.

Mavrose was tied up with what appeared to be golden strings. She was struggling against her bonds – there were spots of blood against the places where the bonds had rubbed her scales raw.

Tight, hot anger lit my chest as I raced over to her; she greeted me a low yowl, silent tears in her eyes and I placed a soft kiss on her snout before rubbing her nose.

DON'T WORRY, I'M COMING!

"I've got you," I murmured and then yanked at the chain.

To my surprise, it came off easily, which was strange, since Mavrose had been yanking against it for the past few hours and it didn't move in the slightest. It occurred to me then that the chains were also probably like the ring – they would not give until *I* removed them, or the purpose of the whole training session would be defeated.

The moment the chains fell away, Mavrose fell to the ground, flopping ungracefully. She was tired, I saw, from extending her senses to the surroundings to direct me, as well as from the magic in the chains that had been holding her back.

I bent down, gently running my hand over the scraped skin of her wounds and frowned.

Suddenly, I heard clapping from behind me. I whirled around to see that the Shahleigh were standing there, looking proud and happy.

I found that I didn't care; I was more concerned about the state of my wounded dragon.

"Well done, Minecraft Steve," Tiamat sounded pleased. "You did it. You passed the second phase of training with flying colors."

"Mavrose is *hurt*!" I protested angrily. "How could you tie her up so?!"

Bazr padded over to us and I glared up at him. He shook his head and bent down to breathe a hot puff of smoke over Mavrose's trembling form.

I watched in shock as her wounds began to close easily, healing themselves quickly. The pain I felt from Mavrose vanished, replaced by warmth and affection as she leapt up and roared her satisfaction to the skies.

"'Tis all a part of the training, child," Soaban offered, "Your challenge was to trust that she would not lead you astray. Hers was to trust that you would free her, both from pain and bondage. It is not an easy thing, for a dragon, to accept the loss of freedom. We are creatures of the sky and to have our wings bound in such a manner is the worst possible fate we can imagine."

"And Ender Dragons feel it most keenly," Tiamat continued, "For they are the fiercest creatures of all, who love the skies more than anything."

"For her to trust you as such," Bazr's tail swished back and forth, "It is truly an honor. You have passed, Minecraft Steve."

I blinked, giddy joy lighting me up from the inside. I turned to Mavrose, who roared a second time, bending down in a silent offering. Grinning widely, I jumped on to her back, settling myself in the familiar space between her shoulders, cryong out in delight as I felt her powerful hind muscles bunch up in anticipation of flight.

"We did it, Mavrose!" I cried, "*We did it!*"

Mavrose leapt – we were in the skies, flying high above the world, letting loose a bright jet of flame into the clouds.

"Silly human," her voice was amused, "I never doubted that we would."

We spent the rest of the day floating above the earth, masters of the sky.

And now, I'm lying curled up against my big, grumpy, sulky Ender Dragon in our quarters, writing down this whole thing.

It's definitely not easy and maybe another dragon species would be safer, but I wouldn't give up training my Ender Dragon for *anything*!

The End

WE DID IT MAVROSE!
SILLY HUMAN, I NEVER DOUBTED THAT WE WOULD!

Special Free Comics Offer From Funny Comics

Funny Comics is the leading publisher of funny stories, comics and graphic novels on the web. Make sure to "LIKE" our fan page on Facebook below:

https://www.facebook.com/FunnyComics3000

On this page we will share news on everything we are up to as well as notify you when our comics and short stories are available for FREE on Kindle.

Other Comics And Short Stories From Funny Comics

DIARY OF A FRIENDLY CREEPER SERIES

In this series of illustrated short stories the Friendly Creeper, as his name implies, just wants to make new friends. However, he is a creeper and as he is constantly reminded, creepers don't make friends! Follow along as the Friendly Creeper strives to become the kind of creeper he wants to be, a friendly one!

Diary Of A Friendly Creeper – School Daze

In Book 1 of the "Diary Of A Friendly Creeper" series a little creeper wakes up one day and decides that, in a most UN-creeper like way that he wants to make some friends. However, he finds this to be most difficult as most of the creatures he meets don't trust him and his creeper family most definitely does not approve. Will the Friendly Creeper be able to actually make any friends or is it just not to be

Diary Of A Friendly Creeper – School Daze

In Book 2 of the "Diary Of A Friendly Creeper" series Friendly Creeper is forced to go to creeper school. At creeper school he is supposed to learn how to scare people and become a proper creeper, everything he doesn't want to do! Can the Friendly Creeper use his new skills to help his friends or will he become just like everyone else

Diary Of A Friendly Creeper – Hobby Hunting

In Book 3 of the "Diary Of A Friendly Creeper" series Friendly Creeper discovers the world of hobbies. Everyone he meets seems to have a hobby of some kind, except for him! Follow along as the Friendly Creeper works to find a hobby of his very own!

Diary Of A Misunderstood Herobrine Series

In this series of illustrated short stories you will get to experience life from Herobrine's point of view. Is Herobrine really bad, or just misunderstood?

<u>Diary Of A Misunderstood Herobrine: It Ain't Easy Being Mean</u>

Everyone knows Herobrine is the villain in Minecraft, but was it always this way? What's more, how did Herobrine get this way to begin with? In this illustrated short story Herobrine tells all from his perspective. At first he really only wanted to build things and help people. However, everyone he meets just won't accept him at his word. Maybe being a bad guy isn't that bad after all?

How To Train Your Ender Dragon Series

In this series of illustrated short stories Steve Montgomery is your typical 15 year old kid with 15 year old problems. However, there is one unusual thing about him. Steve Montgomery has the power to summon dragons ...

Minecraft: How To Train Your Ender Dragon

Steve Montgomery is your typical 15 year old with 15 year old problems. The biggest of which is that he is often bullied by a group of kids that includes his own brother. Steve has something that most other kids don't have, however, for he has the power to summon dragons. After he is literally strung up a flagpole by his tormentors Steve meets a magical dragon who not only saves him but whisks him away to the magical world of Minecraft. However once he arrives there he soon learns that other dangers exist besides school bullies. ...

The MINECRAFT STEVE ADVENTURES
Comic Series

In this fully illustrated comic series Steve must use the power of his imagination in order to defeat the evil plans of Herobrine. We've based stories so far on Jurassic Park, Star Wars and The Wizard Of Oz. More to come!

Minecraft Steve Adventures: Jurassic Block

Minecraft Steve Adventures: Attack On The Death Square

Minecraft Steve Adventures: The Wizard Of IZ

Minecraft Steve Adventures: Your Princess Is In Another Castle

Minecraft Steve Adventures: That's How You Get Ants, Man!

Minecraft Steve Adventures: The Sorcerer's Blunder

The Adventures Of Big Buddy And Little Buddy Comics Series

In this comic series Big Buddy and Little Buddy are friends, inventors and adventurers. Big Buddy tends to be more serious and practical. Little Buddy? Let's just say a little less so. Nonetheless they always have each others back no matter what trouble they get into!

The Adventures Of Big Buddy And Little Buddy – Escape From Planet X

Please Help Us Make Our Comics And Stories Better!

If you enjoy our comics and short stories could you do us a favor and please leave a review on Amazon for them? We gauge a series popularity but how popular it is with our reviewers and readers. The more positive reviews the more likely we are to make more short stories and / or comics in that series. Also, we love hearing from our fans. If you have any ideas / suggestions or improvements please write to us at the e-mail address below. It could be anything. Story ideas, suggestions for improvement, etc. We are thinking about rewarding the top ideas and / or suggestions by perhaps making you a character in a future story. This is only an idea, but we are seriously thinking about it. Anyway, our e-mail address is below:

Funnycomics1@gmail.com

Thank-you again for reading our story and we hope you enjoyed it!

Made in the USA
San Bernardino, CA
11 September 2017